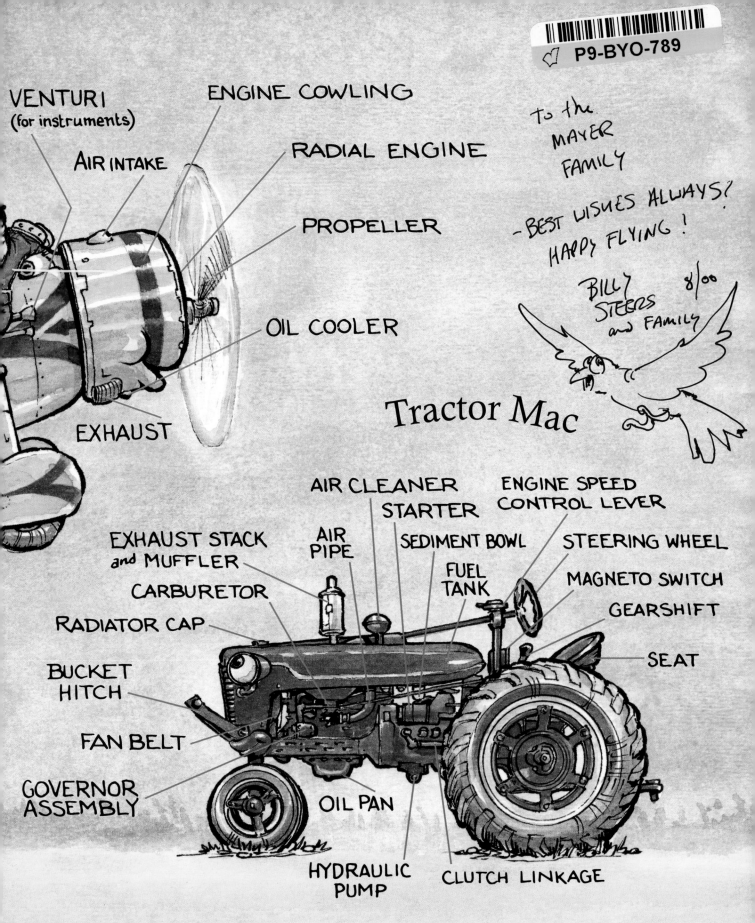

VENTURI
(for instruments)

ENGINE COWLING

AIR INTAKE

RADIAL ENGINE

PROPELLER

OIL COOLER

EXHAUST

To the
MAYER
FAMILY

-BEST WISHES ALWAYS!
HAPPY FLYING!

BILLY
STEERS   8/00
and FAMILY

Tractor Mac

AIR CLEANER
STARTER

ENGINE SPEED
CONTROL LEVER

AIR
PIPE

SEDIMENT BOWL

STEERING WHEEL

EXHAUST STACK
and MUFFLER

FUEL
TANK

MAGNETO SWITCH

CARBURETOR

GEARSHIFT

RADIATOR CAP

SEAT

BUCKET
HITCH

FAN BELT

GOVERNOR
ASSEMBLY

OIL PAN

HYDRAULIC
PUMP

CLUTCH LINKAGE

To Mom and Dad,
who instilled in me the love
to both draw and fly.

Library of Congress Cataloging-in-Publication Data
Steers, Billy.
Tractor Mac learns to fly/ by Billy Steers   p. cm.
Summary: After seeing a plane fly through the sky, Mac the tractor decides that he wants to fly.
ISBN 0-307-10236-X (alk. paper)
[1. Tractors—Fiction. 2. Self-acceptance—Fiction.] I. Title
PZ7.S81536 Tr 2000   [E]—dc21   99-43667

TRACTOR MAC
LEARNS TO FLY

written and illustrated by Billy Steers

A Golden Book * New York

Golden Books Publishing Company, Inc., New York, New York 10106

Tractor Mac and Sibley lived on Stony
Meadow Farm. They shared the work and often
shared their thoughts.

"Do you ever wish you were doing something different, Mac?" asked Sibley one afternoon. "Sometimes I think it would be fun to pull a circus wagon in a parade or maybe a trolley car full of people."

"I am happy just being myself," answered the big red tractor. "Why would I want to be something that I'm not?"

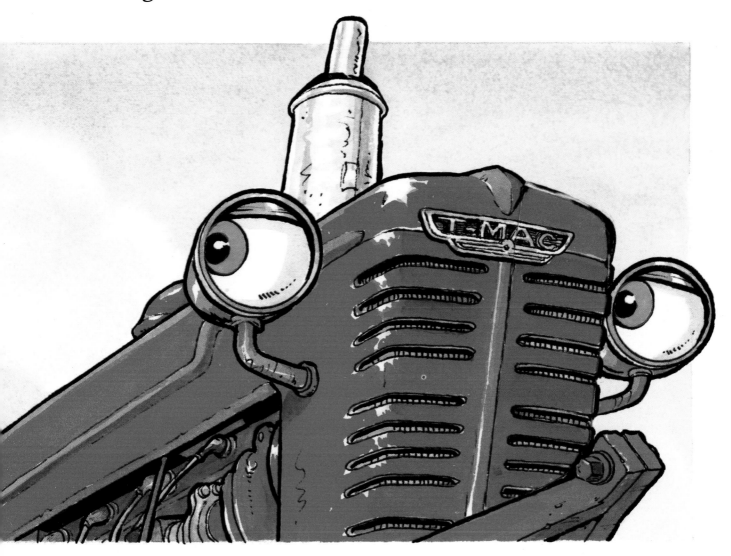

Just then, the two friends heard a sound that
was quite different from Mac's normal chugging
and popping. It roared overhead as it came near.

"Clear the runway!" a bright yellow airplane
shouted as it circled low over their heads.

Tractor Mac stared as the plane bounced to a dusty stop in the hayfield. He had never seen such a beautiful machine.

Smiling passengers climbed out of the yellow
plane while others stood in line to get onboard.
Mac's heart fluttered with excitement. "That
plane gives hayrides in the sky!" he exclaimed.

Mac wheeled over to the yellow plane.
"What's your name?" he asked. "My name is Mac.

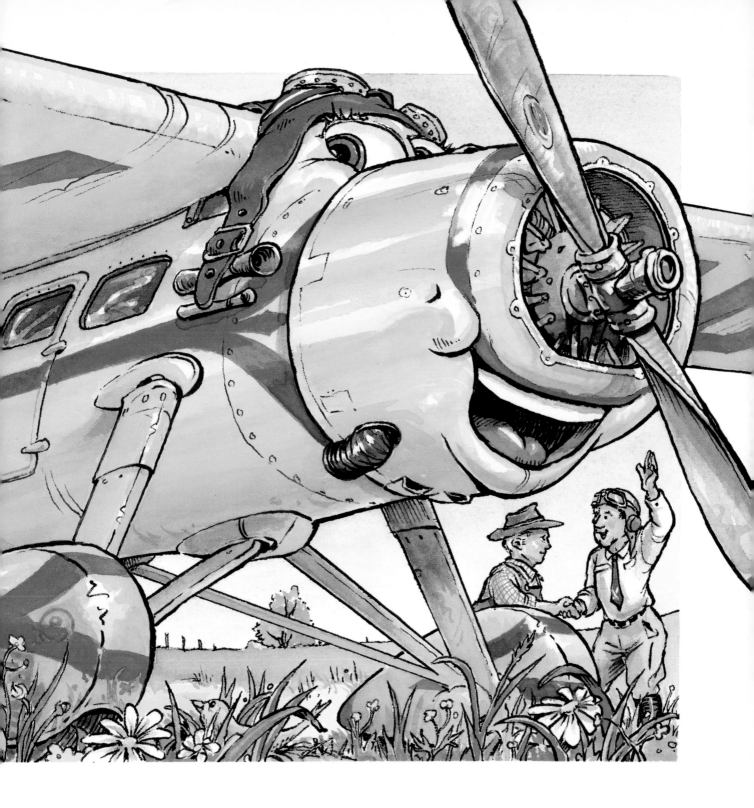

It must be thrilling to fly with the birds. Do you think I could do that?"

"My name is Plane Jane," said the yellow
plane. "And no you couldn't. You don't have any
wings, so how could you fly? Ta ta. Off I go into
the wild blue."

For the rest of the day, all Mac could think
about was flying. What a thrill it must be!

That night, Mac told the story of the bright yellow plane to the birds on the farm. Mac asked them a lot of questions about flying. They talked until late into the night.

Day after day, Mac looked at Plane Jane as she
flew overhead with a new load of thrill seekers.

Soaring, gliding, looping, rolling. As Mac watched, he longed to fly more than ever.

Then one day—quite by accident—Mac's big chance came. As he was chugging down the hill from the pumpkin patch, something snapped. SNORT! PING!

His brakes stopped working. The heavy load pushed Mac faster and faster. He was rolling down the hill out of control!

He could not stop. Zoom!
Suddenly Mac was flying…

for a little while! SPLOOSH!
Mac plunged into the pond.

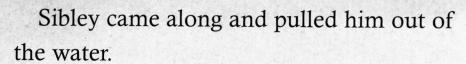
Sibley came along and pulled him out of the water.

"You were right before, Mac," Sibley said. "You should be happy with who you are."

"You bet!" Mac agreed. "Leave the flying for the ducks, geese, and Plane Jane. From now on, my place is with my big black tires planted firmly on the ground."

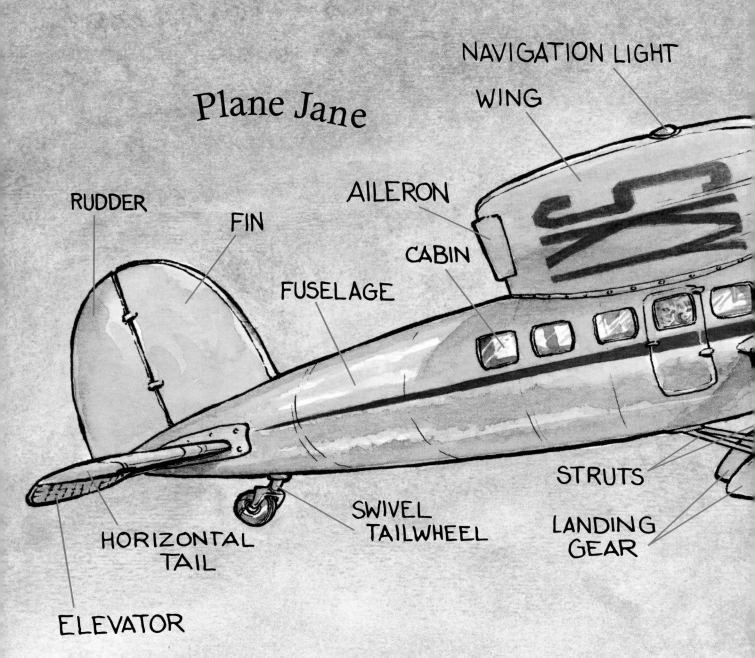

Plane Jane

NAVIGATION LIGHT

WING

RUDDER

FIN

AILERON

CABIN

FUSELAGE

STRUTS

HORIZONTAL
TAIL

SWIVEL
TAILWHEEL

LANDING
GEAR

ELEVATOR